Bunch

...NTED
SLEEPOVER

by Nancy K. Wallace
illustrated by Amanda Chronister

visit us at www.abdopublishing.com

For my husband, Dennie, and my original Book Bunch: Hanna, Derrick, & Dakota
—NW

Published by Magic Wagon, a division of the ABDO Group, PO Box 398166, Minneapolis, MN 55439.

Calico Chapter Books™ is a trademark and logo of Magic Wagon.

Printed in the United States of America, North Mankato, Minnesota.
102012
012013

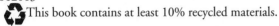This book contains at least 10% recycled materials.

Text by Nancy K. Wallace
Illustrations by Amanda Chronister
Edited by Stephanie Hedlund and Rochelle Baltzer
Layout and design by Neil Klinepier

Library of Congress Cataloging-in-Publication Data
Wallace, Nancy K.
  The haunted sleepover / by Nancy K. Wallace ; illustrated by Amanda Chronister.
    p. cm. -- (Abby and the Book Bunch)
  Summary: Christmas is almost here, and the Christmas sleepover at the public library may be canceled because strange noises in the library cellar have led to rumors that the library is haunted--so Abby and her friends set out to catch a ghost.
  ISBN 978-1-61641-913-4
  1. Public libraries--Juvenile fiction. 2. Books and reading--Juvenile fiction. 3. Sleepovers--Juvenile fiction. 4. Flying squirrels--Juvenile fiction. 5. Christmas stories. [1. Public libraries--Fiction. 2. Books and reading--Fiction. 3. Sleepovers--Fiction. 4. Flying squirrels--Fiction. 5. Squirrels--Fiction. 6. Christmas--Fiction. 7. Mystery and detective stories.] I. Chronister, Amanda, ill. II. Title.
PZ7.W158752Hau 2013
813.6--dc23
                                                    2012029414

CONTENTS

Holiday Spirits

"Do you believe in ghosts?" Abby asked her best friend, Sydney.

Everyone stopped talking at their lunch table. They all turned to look at Abby.

Dakota snorted. He pulled his sweatshirt up over his head. He wiggled his fingers at Abby pretending to grab her.

"Do you?" he asked in a spooky voice.

Abby rolled her eyes. It was the second week of December. Their third-grade teacher, Mr. Kim, was reading *A Christmas Carol* to their class.

"I'm not sure," Abby said. "But I think Marley's ghost is pretty scary."

Dakota pulled his sweatshirt back down. His hair stood on end, but he didn't seem to care. "It's just a story," he said, munching his sandwich.

"It is kind of scary," Sydney admitted. "I don't like all those chains clanking!"

Zachary banged his chair into the table leg. "Look out! Marley is coming after you!" he yelled.

"I'll come after you if you don't be quiet!" said Sydney.

5

Zachary put two carrot sticks under his top lip. He grinned. "Be afraid," he said. "Be very afraid!"

Sydney looked at Abby. She shook her head. "Poor Zachary, he's stuck in the wrong month. He thinks it's still Halloween."

"I wish it was Halloween!" Zachary said. "That's my favorite holiday!"

"I like Christmas better," Abby said.

"So do I," said Sydney. "Christmas has sparkly lights and lots of decorations. And I love cookies and hot cocoa!"

"Christmas presents are awesome!" Dakota said. "I asked for skis this year!"

"And I love snow!" said Abby. She bit into her apple. "Snow is the best part of winter! I hope you can use your skis. We haven't had one single flake yet."

Sydney patted her shoulder. "Mr. Kim is going to let us cut out snowflakes this afternoon," she said. "We'll make our own snow. We can tape it on the windows!"

"He has a tree, too," Dakota said. "I saw the box in the hall."

"And tomorrow night we get to trim the big tree at the library!" Abby said. She and her friends liked to help out at Evergreen Public Library. Mrs. Mackenzie, the children's librarian, called them Abby and the Book Bunch. She always found fun jobs for them!

"What time are you going to the library?" Dakota asked.

"My mom is dropping Sydney and me off at five thirty," Abby said. "The Christmas ornaments are in the library's cellar. We promised to carry them up. Mrs. Mackenzie said there were four big boxes."

"Aren't you afraid to go down in that cellar?" Dakota asked. "They say it's haunted!"

Zachary grinned. "Hey, that's cool!" he said.

"It is not haunted!" Abby protested.

Sydney leaned forward. "Who told you that, Dakota?" she asked.

Dakota shrugged. "I don't remember. Somebody did. It's supposed to be haunted by some old librarian. She walks around hunting for a lost book."

Sydney looked disgusted. "Dakota, that is just stupid!" she said.

But Abby was worried. "Books do get lost at the library," she pointed out.

"But ghosts don't come looking for them!" Sydney protested. "Don't listen to him, Abby. He's just trying to scare you."

Dakota sat back with a satisfied grin. "Wait until tomorrow night and we'll see who's right. It gets dark very early this time of year. Who knows what is waiting down in that creepy old cellar?"

Sydney threw a piece of bread at Dakota. "Go bother someone else!" she said.

Dakota laughed. "Why?" he asked. "Bothering you is so much fun!"

Abby didn't laugh. She thought about the cellar at the library. She had only been down there once. It was dark and cold and it smelled funny. Now she wasn't sure she wanted to go down there.

Things That Go Bump in the Night

It was dark when Sydney and Abby arrived at the library. Wreaths hung in all the windows. Pine trees stood on each side of the double doors. They were covered with twinkle lights.

"The library looks pretty," Sydney said.

"It would look prettier with snow," said Abby. "Last year we had snow for Thanksgiving. This year we have had rain, rain, rain."

"It will snow," said Sydney. "Just wait."

"I'm tired of waiting," Abby protested.

Mrs. Mackenzie was on her knees by the circulation desk. She was setting up a snowman. He had twinkle lights on his hat. She shivered as the door closed.

"Hi, girls!" Mrs. Mackenzie said. "It's really cold in here! We got a big delivery of books this afternoon. So, we had the door propped open."

Sydney smiled. "It just feels like Christmas!"

"It doesn't look like Christmas," Abby said. "There's no snow!"

"It looks like Christmas in here," Mrs. Mackenzie said. "I'm glad you hung those snowflakes from the ceiling last week. They look great!"

Abby looked up. The paper snowflakes sparkled with glitter. They danced back and forth every time the doors opened.

"They do look really nice," Abby said.

"Wow!" said Sydney. "Look at that tree!"

The library Christmas tree was huge. It stood right in the center of the library.

"It's beautiful!" said Abby. The tree was pretty even without any ornaments.

Its dark green needles made the whole library smell like pine.

"My husband brought it in this afternoon," Mrs. Mackenzie said. "I was afraid it might be too big. But it is just perfect. We'll need a ladder to decorate it."

"We came to help you get the decorations out of the cellar," Abby said.

"I have to stay at the desk for a while. Can you two get them alone?" Mrs. Mackenzie asked. She handed Abby her keys.

Abby loved to have Mrs. Mackenzie's keys. They always made her feel important. But she wasn't sure she wanted to go down in the cellar without an adult.

Sydney nudged Abby. "We know where everything is," she said. "Let's go, Abby!"

Mrs. Mackenzie called after them. "Be sure to turn the lights off in the cellar when you are done!"

Abby and Sydney walked to the very back of the library. They stopped in front of a door that said "Staff Only." Abby pushed the door open. The hall was dark.

"Where is the light switch?" Sydney asked.

"It's a motion detector light," Abby said.

Abby stepped into the hall. The light switched on. It showed the dusty steps leading down to the cellar. The stairway was full of shadows.

"This is creepy," Abby said.

"It's just dark," Sydney said. "Come on!"

"It's dark and creepy," Abby said. She didn't touch the dusty railing.

"How old do you think the library is?" Sydney asked.

"Really old," Abby said. "Gram says it's the oldest building in town."

They reached the bottom of the steps. Abby turned on the cellar lights.

Three lightbulbs hung from the ceiling. Old wooden shelves lined the brick walls. Boxes were stacked in every corner. File cabinet drawers bulged with paper. Sheets covered old furniture.

Sydney pointed to a wobbly table in the center of the room. "The Christmas things are over there," she said. "I saw them when we put the Halloween stuff away."

Something moved in the back corner.

"Did you hear that?" Abby asked.

Sydney nodded. She took a step backward. "Just grab the Christmas boxes," she said. "Let's go back upstairs."

"I told you it was creepy down here," Abby said. She picked up a box of ornaments.

Sydney took a box, too.

There were still two boxes left. "We'll have to make two trips," Abby said.

"I don't want to come down here again," Sydney said.

"We could just put all of them on the steps," Abby said. "Then we won't have to come back into the cellar."

Suddenly Sydney pointed at the ceiling. "Look at that!"

One of the lights was swinging back and forth.

"Why is it doing that?" Abby whispered. She moved closer to Sydney. "What if the library really is haunted?"

"I don't believe in ghosts," Sydney said.

"Then why is that light swinging?" Abby asked.

"I don't know," said Sydney. "Let's get out of here!"

Crash! Something smashed onto the floor in the back corner.

"Run!" Sydney yelled.

Ghosts of Librarians Past

Abby and Sydney ran all the way to the circulation desk.

"Mrs. Mackenzie!" Abby gasped.

"What's the matter?" Mrs. Mackenzie asked. "You girls look like you've seen a ghost!"

"We heard a noise!" Abby cried.

"And the light was swinging!" Sydney yelled.

"Someone is in the cellar!" Abby finished.

"Oh my!" said Mrs. Mackenzie. "I'll go right down!"

Abby and Sydney ran ahead of her. Abby opened the door to the hall. It didn't look quite so spooky with Mrs. Mackenzie right behind them.

Mrs. Mackenzie hurried down the cellar steps. She stopped at the bottom. The decorations were scattered on the floor. "Who's here?" she asked. Her voice trembled.

Abby didn't hear a sound. The lights hung absolutely still.

"Something fell down," Abby said, pointing. "Over there in the back."

Mrs. Mackenzie walked into the shadows. She bent over. "There are books on the floor," she said. "Did you girls bump them?"

Sydney was standing by the table. "We were up here when it happened," she said.

Mrs. Mackenzie walked back toward the girls. She had a crumbling book in her hand. "This is an old book," she said. She turned the pages carefully. "The copyright is 1850."

"That's really old!" Abby said.

"I think the library was built in 1850," said Mrs. Mackenzie. "This must be one of its first books."

"Who was the first librarian?" Abby asked.

"There's a picture of her down here," Mrs. Mackenzie said. She looked along the wall. Her hand reached for an old picture hanging on a nail.

The dusty glass made the picture hard to see. Mrs. Mackenzie picked up a rag. She wiped the glass. "There she is," she said.

Abby looked at the woman in the picture. Her gray hair was pulled back into a bun. Her glasses sat on the very end of her nose. She was frowning. Abby made a face. "She doesn't look very friendly."

Mrs. Mackenzie laughed. "I wouldn't want to tell her I had an overdue book!"

"She looks mean," Sydney said.

"Maybe she didn't want to have her picture taken," said Mrs. Mackenzie. "Or maybe she was just having a bad day."

"What was her name?" Abby asked.

Mrs. Mackenzie turned the picture over. She dusted it off with her rag. "Her name was Gertrude Stern," she said.

Abby giggled. "Her last name was really *Stern*?" she asked.

"That's so funny!" Sydney said.

Mrs. Mackenzie wasn't laughing. Her face looked white.

"Are you okay?" Abby asked.

Mrs. Mackenzie nodded. "Yes," she said. "It's just that when I first started to work here, I heard stories about Miss Stern."

Abby's heart was pounding. "What kind of stories?" she asked.

Mrs. Mackenzie patted Abby's shoulder. "They were just silly stories. Everyone joked that Miss Stern haunted the library. She was supposed to be looking for a lost book."

Abby pointed to the leather book. "Maybe that's it," she said. "Maybe you found it."

"Maybe I did," Mrs. Mackenzie said. She picked up the book. "I'll take it upstairs with me. Now tell me what happened when you came down here."

"The light at that end started to swing," Sydney said. "And then those books fell down."

"Hmmm," said Mrs. Mackenzie. "Well, there is no one here now. Maybe a draft made the light swing."

All three of them looked at the ceiling. All the lights hung motionless.

"Then why wouldn't all of them swing?" asked Abby.

"I don't know," said Mrs. Mackenzie.

"And who knocked the books on the floor?" asked Sydney.

Mrs. Mackenzie shivered. "I don't know that either," she said. "Let's go back upstairs now. Can each of you carry a box of decorations? I'll get the last two."

Abby took one last look around the cellar. Mrs. Mackenzie turned out the cellar lights. They started up the stairs. Then Abby heard something go *tap, tap, tap* in the dark behind them.

"Did you hear that?" Abby asked.

Mrs. Mackenzie nodded. "I'll send Art down when he comes. I'm not going back down there tonight."

Abby wished Art, the janitor, was there right now! She remembered what Dakota had told her. Maybe he was right. Maybe Miss Stern did haunt the library. Abby walked faster.

Tap, tap, tap! The noise seemed to follow them up the stairs.

Trim the Tree

Dakota and Zachary were waiting upstairs by the Christmas tree when Abby, Sydney, and Mrs. Mackenzie arrived.

Abby ran to meet them. "We just heard something scary in the cellar!" she cried.

An older man looked up from his newspaper.

Abby lowered her voice. She and Sydney told the boys what had happened.

"All the exciting stuff happens when I'm not here!" Zachary complained.

Dakota was hopping up and down with excitement. "Let's go down and investigate!" he said. "Give me the keys, Abby."

"No!" Mrs. Mackenzie said. "No one else is going to the cellar. I'll have Art check it out when he comes in."

"Shoot!" Dakota grumbled. "The library has a real ghost. And you won't let me see it!"

The man put his newspaper down. He stared at Dakota and Abby.

Mrs. Mackenzie's face was still pale. "It's not a ghost, Dakota," she whispered.

"We're having the Christmas Sleepover soon. All the kids will be afraid to come! Please don't tell people the library is haunted."

"But what if it is?" Dakota demanded.

Mrs. Mackenzie turned away. "It's not," she replied. "It's probably just a mouse in the cellar. Can you set up the tables for the refreshments, please?"

Dakota looked at the floor. "Sure," he said.

Abby and Sydney got tablecloths and napkins. The boys moved tables. No one talked. They weren't allowed to talk about ghosts. And they couldn't think of anything else to talk about.

Abby and Sydney put cookies on trays for the tree-trimming party. They opened the boxes of ornaments. Abby looked toward the cellar door. Everything was quiet.

The man with the newspaper left. Maybe the party preparations scared him away.

By six thirty, the library was filled with people. Children tumbled through the library doors. Their faces were red with cold. Abby helped put coats and mittens on a table.

Everyone laughed and talked. They all loved the huge Christmas tree! Abby began to relax. The library seemed warm and cozy again. Maybe it was just a mouse in the cellar!

Decorating the tree was fun. Dakota and Zachary zipped up and down the ladder. They hung ornaments on the highest branches. They put a star on the very top of the pine. Every single branch had an ornament.

The tree shimmered and glittered when they were finished. Abby gathered the empty boxes. She slid them under the table.

Mrs. Mackenzie brought out hot cocoa. Everyone ate lots of cookies while they admired the tree. They all sat down in a circle after they ate.

"Now it's time for 'The Twelve Days of Christmas!'" Mrs. Mackenzie said.

Everyone laughed and stood up again. Mrs. Mackenzie sang the song every year at the Christmas party. She made up funny motions for each verse.

People stood on one leg for the partridge. They flapped their arms for the French hens. Everyone pretended to play flutes for the pipers piping. They spun around for the ladies dancing.

Dakota crashed into Sydney and Abby. Zachary fell down. He rolled around on the floor and laughed. Abby giggled so hard she couldn't sing. Finally it was over!

People laughed and collapsed in their chairs. Mrs. Mackenzie picked up a book with Santa on the cover. She always ended the party with *The Night Before Christmas.* Everyone waited quietly for her to begin.

Abby saw smiling faces everywhere she looked. The library tree was beautiful. Everyone was having lots of fun. It had been a perfect Christmas party. Abby grinned at Sydney.

Mrs. Mackenzie began reading. Abby glanced out the window. Christmas lights glittered in the dark. *Now if only there were snowflakes falling,* she thought. *Then everything would be perfect!*

Rumors

Sydney slept at Abby's house on Friday night. They watched Christmas specials on TV. Abby's mom made popcorn. All night they could hear rain on the roof.

On Saturday morning, the sun was shining. It was windy and mild.

"We'd better put up those Christmas lights," Abby's dad said. "It's not going to be warm forever."

"Is it supposed to get colder?" Abby asked hopefully.

Her dad ruffled her hair. "It's December. It's bound to get colder. You just have to be patient."

They had blueberry pancakes for breakfast. Then Abby and Sydney helped Abby's dad decorate. They carried lights and pine out to the porch.

"What are you wearing for the sleepover?" Sydney asked.

"I'm going to wear my Christmas pajamas," Abby said. She untangled a string of lights and handed it to Sydney.

"Me too!" Sydney replied. She wound the lights around the pine garland. "I always get new pajamas on Christmas Eve."

"I do too," said Abby. "Sometimes I even get slippers!"

Abby's dad leaned down from the ladder. He held out his hand. "I need a hammer," he said.

Abby's golden retriever, Lucy, jumped up to lick him. "Just what I need," he said, "a little doggie drool!" He wiped his hand on his pants.

"I'll go get the hammer," Abby said. She glanced at the sky. Today it felt like spring. It was so warm. No snow and Christmas was just one week away!

Her father laughed. "Stop looking for snowflakes! I need that hammer!" he said.

"I'm going!" Abby said. She opened the front door and ran to the kitchen. Her mom and Gram were baking cookies. The house smelled like Christmas.

Gingerbread men covered the kitchen table. Abby's mom was icing them. Gram was adding candy eyes.

"Oh, those look so good!" Abby said. "Can I have one?"

Her mom smiled. She had flour on one cheek. "Yes! Take one for Sydney and Dad, too. How is the porch coming?" she asked.

Abby bit into a big gingerbread man. It tasted spicy and sweet. "Dad needs a hammer," she said.

"It's in the drawer by the sink," her mom said. "I'll make hot cocoa when you're done."

Abby grabbed the hammer in one hand. She took two cookies in the other. She ran back to the porch. "Here is the hammer!" she said. She handed it to her dad.

Her dad eyed the cookies. "What do you have there?" he asked.

Abby held them up. "Cookies for you and Sydney," she said.

Lucy jumped at Abby's hand. She grabbed the cookies and scarfed them down. "Lucy, no!" Abby cried. Only crumbs fell on the porch.

Abby's dad laughed. "I hope Mom has some more."

"She does," Abby said. "Lucy, that was bad!"

Lucy just wagged her tail. She smiled a doggie smile.

"I'll go get some more," said Abby. She walked back into the house. Gram was reading the paper. "I need more cookies," Abby said.

"They must be very hungry!" her mom said.

"Lucy ate them!" Abby said. "She grabbed them right out of my hand!"

Gram looked up. "Abby, do you know anything about this?" she asked. "Dakota is quoted in this article."

"What article?" Abby asked.

Abby walked around the table. Gram pointed at the front page. The headline read "Ghost Haunts Local Library."

"The reporter interviewed Dakota," Gram said. "Dakota said that two of his friends saw a ghost. It's supposed to haunt the cellar of the library."

"Oh no!" said Abby. "Mrs. Mackenzie is going to be so mad!"

Ghosts and Poltergeists

Abby walked to school Monday morning. The sun shone brightly. The air felt just like spring. The decorations on the lampposts looked funny and out of place.

It should be snowing, she thought.

Dakota was just getting off the bus.

Abby thought about the newspaper article. She ran up to him. "How could you do that?" Abby asked angrily.

Dakota wheeled around to look at her. "How could I do what?" he asked. "What's the matter?"

"I'm sure Mrs. Mackenzie is really upset with you!" Abby said. "Everyone will think the library is haunted because of that newspaper story. No one will be allowed to go to the sleepover!"

Dakota grinned. "I'm allowed to go," he said. "So is Zachary. I hope we get to see the ghost!"

Kids streamed past them toward the school. Several of them stopped to listen.

Abby threw her hands in the air. "We didn't see a ghost!" she protested. "We saw a light swing. Then some books fell on the floor."

Dakota frowned. "But you said the cellar was creepy. You were scared when you came upstairs."

"I was scared because we heard funny noises," Abby said. "I didn't see a ghost!"

"Well, it might have been a ghost," Dakota said. He rummaged in his backpack. "Look at this book. It tells about poltergeists."

"What's a poltergeist?" asked Abby.

"A kind of spirit," said Dakota. "They throw things and make funny noises."

Abby rolled her eyes. "Why would a poltergeist be in the library?" she asked.

"They can be anywhere!" Dakota said. "They try to scare people. They do mischievous things."

Abby laughed. "That is a very big word for you!"

"It says that in this book," Dakota said. He held the title up for her to see. The book was called *Ghosts and Evil Spirits*.

Abby frowned. "Evil spirits?" she said. "Are poltergeists evil?"

Dakota shook his head. "No, they just do bad things."

"Kind of like you," Abby said. "You aren't evil. You just do bad things!" They started up the steps to the school.

"It wasn't my fault!" Dakota protested. "That reporter asked me about the ghost. He heard us talking in the library. He waited for me after the party."

"Well, you shouldn't have said we saw a ghost," Abby told him. "We didn't! And now everyone thinks the library is haunted!"

"I can't change the story now," Dakota said.

Abby stopped. She had an idea. "No, but we could find out the truth. Something made those noises. Maybe we can find out what it was."

"How will that help?" Dakota asked.

"If we know what really happened, we could call the newspaper," Abby said. "Maybe they would write another story."

"Do you really think so?" Dakota asked.

Abby shrugged. "It's worth a try."

"I'll help you," said Dakota. "When can we start?"

"We'll start right after school," Abby said. "I told Mrs. Mackenzie that I'd put books away."

"Okay, I'll come with you," said Dakota.

Abby tapped his chest with her finger. "And you need to apologize," she said. "It will be your fault if the sleepover is canceled!"

"You think they would do that?" he asked. "Everyone loves the Christmas Sleepover!"

"They will have to cancel it if no one signs up!" said Abby. "You and I have to fix this somehow. Now, come on. We're going to be late for school!"

Lights Out!

The library was very quiet after school. The newspaper reporter was reading at a table. His camera dangled around his neck. He looked up when Abby and Dakota walked in. They ignored him.

They went to look for Mrs. Mackenzie. But the Children's Area was empty. The toys and books were neatly put away. They found Mrs. Mackenzie in her office.

"Is Story Time over for the year?" Abby asked.

"Yes," Mrs. Mackenzie said. She laid some paper Christmas stockings on her desk. "Today was the last one. I only had three kids. Hardly anyone came."

"I'm sorry!" Abby said. She had helped cut out the stockings. They had put a lot of work into them.

Mrs. Mackenzie forced a smile. "I'll save the stockings for next year," she said. She held out a jar of candy canes. "Would you like one? I have a lot left over."

"Thanks," said Abby. She took a striped candy cane. "Maybe everyone was busy today. There is so much to do before Christmas!"

Dakota dug his toe into the floor. He didn't look at Mrs. Mackenzie. "Or maybe everyone read the newspaper," he said. "Maybe they were afraid to come."

Mrs. Mackenzie sighed. "You might be right, Dakota. Two more newspapers have called about the story. A TV news crew was filming the library when I came to work."

"That's awful!" Abby said.

Mrs. Mackenzie sat down at her desk. "That's not the worst part," she said. "We've already had ten cancellations for the sleepover. The director may cancel it."

"No!" Abby wailed. "Please don't cancel the sleepover! We love it!"

"I can't have a sleepover for half a dozen kids," Mrs. Mackenzie said.

"I'm sorry," Dakota said. "I shouldn't have talked to that reporter." He hung his head. "Or I should have been careful about what I said."

"All of this is your fault," Abby said. "You should have told the truth."

"Everyone makes mistakes, Abby," Mrs. Mackenzie said. She patted Dakota's shoulder. "It's okay, Dakota. It's done. Let's just hope people forget about it."

"We think maybe we can help," Abby said.

"Yeah," said Dakota. "We want to investigate!"

Mrs. Mackenzie frowned. "You want to investigate the ghost?" she asked.

Dakota grinned. "Maybe it's not a ghost. We can find out what it really is!"

Mrs. Mackenzie shook her head. "I don't know," she said.

"Then we can tell the newspaper the truth," Abby said. "And everyone will know that the library isn't haunted!"

Mrs. Mackenzie looked doubtful. "I think the damage is already done. People believe what they read in the paper."

"Maybe they will write another story," Abby begged. "Please let us go down to the cellar again."

"I don't think that's a good idea," Mrs. Mackenzie said. "I don't want anyone to get hurt."

"We won't get hurt!" Dakota said.

"Strange things have been happening," Mrs. Mackenzie said. "We've heard more noises. And food was taken from the breakroom."

Tap, tap, tap! Abby heard a familiar sound. She looked up at the ceiling above her head. *Tap, tap, tap!* She heard it again.

Then, the lights went off! The computer screens went black.

"Oh no!" groaned Mrs. Mackenzie. "What's happening now?"

The emergency lights snapped on all over the library. Mrs. Mackenzie went to the circulation desk. Abby and Dakota went with her.

People had gathered together. Everyone was wondering what had happened.

"There must have been a power failure," Mrs. Mackenzie said.

Dakota looked out the window. "The lights are on across the street," he said.

"Maybe we blew a fuse then," Mrs. Mackenzie explained. "This is an old building."

"Or maybe it's the ghost," said the reporter.

Someone laughed.

"There isn't a ghost!" Mrs. Mackenzie protested.

"That's not what I was told," said the reporter. He looked straight at Dakota.

Suddenly, the main lights flickered. They stayed on.

"There," said Mrs. Mackenzie with a smile. "It seems to be fixed! Now we'll get these computers back online."

Mrs. Mackenzie turned to Abby. She held out her keys. "Go ahead," she whispered. "See what you can find. But you come right upstairs if anything strange happens."

"Okay," said Abby. "Come on, Dakota. Let's solve a mystery!"

The Thing in the Cellar

Abby and Dakota went to the back of the library. Abby put the key in the lock. She looked at Dakota. She took a deep breath and opened the door. The hall light was already on.

"That's funny," Abby said.

Dakota frowned. "What?" he asked.

"The light is on," Abby said.

Dakota shook his head. "All the lights came back on," he reminded her.

"But this one is a motion detector light," Abby explained. "It only comes on when someone walks into the hall."

"Oh," Dakota said in a small voice. He stepped forward and peeked down the stairs. "Maybe someone is already down there."

"The door was locked," Abby said.

"Then why was the light on?" Dakota asked. He took a step back. "Maybe we shouldn't go down."

Abby put her hands on her hips. "Do you want to have the sleepover or not?"

"I do," Dakota said. He sighed. "Let's go."

They crept down the stairs. The cellar below them was quiet until they reached the bottom step.

Tap, tap, tap!

"Did you hear that?" Abby whispered.

"Yeah," Dakota replied softly. "What do you think it is?"

"I don't know," Abby said. Her hands were shaking. She reached for the cellar light switch. "Are you ready?" she whispered.

Dakota nodded.

Abby switched the lights on. There was a scrambling noise. A box hit the floor with a bang. Something skittered into the shadows.

"What was that?" Dakota asked.

Abby shook her head. "I couldn't see. But I think it's still here."

Dakota pulled Abby back toward the steps. "Abby, what if someone's living down here? Mrs. Mackenzie said there was food missing. Maybe we should go back upstairs."

Abby's heart was pounding. She didn't look at Dakota. "You can go if you want to," she said.

Dakota shuffled his feet. "I'm not going to leave you alone," he said finally.

Abby exhaled. "Thanks," she said. "Come on."

The cellar didn't look very different. A box lay on its side in the middle of the floor. Bookends had spilled out onto the cement. Abby and Dakota walked around them.

They edged closer to the back of the room. Boxes towered above them. Abby looked at the shelves along the wall. Nothing seemed to be out of place. Cobwebs draped the pictures on the walls.

Dakota pointed. "Look," he said.

An old blanket lay folded on top of a box of books. The edges were ragged. The blanket looked lumpy.

Abby made a face. "Maybe you are right," she whispered. "Maybe someone is living down here."

Dakota reached for the edge of the blanket.

"Don't pick it up!" Abby protested. "It's all dusty and dirty!"

"I want to know what's under it," Dakota said. He picked up the edge of the blanket. Under it were two cookies and some peanuts. Empty candy wrappers rolled onto the floor.

Dakota looked at Abby. "I'll bet those came from the breakroom," he said.

Something rustled in the shadows. The sound of tiny footsteps moved closer. Abby and Dakota backed toward the door.

—

The Chase

Suddenly a dark shape swooped down from the shelves. Abby covered her eyes and screamed! *Chuck, chuck, chuck!* A loud chattering filled the cellar.

Dakota started to laugh. "It's a squirrel!" he said.

Abby peeked out from behind her hands. A small, reddish squirrel stood on the box. It had very large eyes. Its feet stamped furiously on the blanket.

It looked so funny that Abby had to laugh, too. "It thinks we are going to take its food," she said.

"Well, there's your library ghost!" said Dakota.

"But no one will believe us!" Abby said. "We'll have to catch it."

The squirrel leaped up onto a shelf. "That's not going to be easy," said Dakota.

"Maybe we could throw the blanket over it," Abby suggested.

"We can try," Dakota said. He grabbed the blanket, scattering the cookies and peanuts.

The squirrel stamped its feet in rage. It raced back and forth on the shelf chattering.

Dakota threw the blanket at the shelf. The squirrel sailed over their heads. It landed on one of the picture frames. It tilted crazily but the squirrel hung on.

"How does it do that?" Abby said.

"I don't know," Dakota said. "It's like it can fly! It's really fast!"

Dakota gathered up the blanket again. He aimed at the squirrel and threw it. The squirrel slid off the picture. It streaked between Abby's feet.

Abby squealed and jumped up onto the table. Dakota raced past her. The squirrel zoomed back toward Dakota. Dakota screamed and ran the other way.

"Help!" Dakota yelled.

The squirrel dashed up the front of the shelves. It perched on the highest one and chattered loudly at them.

Abby heard footsteps on the stairs. Art appeared at the door. "What's going on in here?" he asked.

Abby and Dakota started to laugh. They laughed so hard they could hardly talk. Finally, Abby pointed at the shelves. "There's a squirrel," she said.

"We tried to catch it," Dakota added. "But it's too fast!"

Art looked at the squirrel. "What did you try to catch it with?" he asked.

Dakota waved the blanket and giggled. "This," he said.

Art shook his head. "You need a trap," he said.

"But it's so cute!" Abby protested.

"It won't be cute if it chews the wiring," Art said. "Mrs. Mackenzie has been having trouble with the lights. I'll bet that little guy is the problem."

"Just don't hurt it," Abby said.

"I won't hurt it," Art said. "I'm just going to catch it. You kids stay right there. Keep an eye on it. I'll be back in a minute."

Abby climbed down from the table. The squirrel paced back and forth above their heads. Its feet danced on the shelf. *Tap, tap, tap!*

"See," said Abby. "That's the noise Sydney and I heard. It was the squirrel all along."

"I hope that reporter is still here," Dakota said. "Now we can give him the real story!"

Art came back with the trap. It was long and narrow with a door at each end. Art put the peanuts and cookies inside. Then he took part of a peanut butter sandwich and put it in, too.

"See?" Art said. "I'm even giving it part of my lunch." He closed the trap door. "Now," Art said, "can you kids be real quiet?"

Abby and Dakota nodded.

"Go sit on the stairs," Art said. "I'm going to turn out the cellar lights."

Abby and Dakota sat down on the steps. Art turned out the lights. He sat beside them. He put a finger to his lips. They each held their breath and waited.

Success!

Abby, Dakota, and Art sat on the stairs for a long time. Nothing happened. Then the door upstairs opened.

"Is everything all right?" Mrs. Mackenzie called down.

"Shhh," Art whispered back. "Everything is just fine. We'll be up in a little while."

The door closed again. They sat in silence. The cellar was quiet. The squirrel must have been waiting for them to leave.

Abby looked at the dust on the railing. She drew a snowflake in it.

Dakota smiled. He drew a tic-tac-toe game on the steps. They played four games. Dakota won every time!

Thump! Something moved in the cellar. The squirrel must have jumped down from the shelves. He skittered across the floor. His little feet went *tap, tap, tap* as he ran.

Art smiled and wiggled his eyebrows. They all sat very still.

The squirrel ran back and forth. Abby imagined him circling the cage.

Snap! The trap door slammed shut!

"Got it!" Art said with a grin. "Now we can take it outside where it belongs."

Abby stood up. "But first," she said, "we have to show it to Mrs. Mackenzie!"

Art flipped on the light switch. The squirrel began chattering. Its feet drummed on the cage floor.

"Can I carry it?" Dakota asked.

"All right," said Art. "But don't put your fingers inside. It'll bite."

Dakota carefully grabbed the cage. Together, Art, Abby, Dakota, and the squirrel went upstairs.

Mrs. Mackenzie came running to meet them. "What is that?" she asked.

"This is your ghost," Art said. "It's only a squirrel."

"It's a very strange-looking squirrel," Mrs. Mackenzie said. "I never saw one with such big eyes. And it's very small. Is it a baby?"

"It's a flying squirrel," Art said. "They're not very big."

"I'll look for a book about them," said Mrs. Mackenzie. "Maybe we can find out more about this little troublemaker!"

Abby looked at the squirrel in the light. It wasn't very big. But it sure had caused a lot of trouble!

"I'll bet it's been chewing on the wiring," Art said. "You'd better have an electrician check it out."

"I'll call one right away," said Mrs. Mackenzie.

"How did the squirrel get in the library?" Abby asked. "Was it hiding in the Christmas tree?"

"I don't think so," Art said. He nodded at Mrs. Mackenzie. "These ladies prop the door open when they get deliveries. All it had to do was run right in!"

Mrs. Mackenzie laughed. "I guess we'll have to be more careful. What are you going to do with it now?"

"I'll let it loose outside," said Art. "I hope it doesn't come back. It seems to like the library!"

"Don't let it go yet," said Abby. "There is someone else I want to show him to. Come on, Dakota."

Dakota grinned. Together they carried the squirrel to the reading area. The newspaper reporter was in for a surprise!

Front-page News

It was the day before Christmas. Abby ran downstairs. She turned on the lights on the Christmas tree. She plugged in the lights on the mantel, too.

Christmas music was coming from the kitchen. Abby ran in. Her mom was making coffee. Gram was unfolding the newspaper.

"Merry Christmas!" Abby said.

Her mom turned around and smiled. "Merry Christmas!" she said.

"Well," said Gram. "Look at this!" She spread the paper out on the table so everyone could see it.

The headline was very big. It said, "Kids Nab Squirrel at Library." There was a picture of Abby and Dakota on the front page! They were holding the flying squirrel's cage between them.

"Wow!" Abby said.

Gram adjusted her glasses. She began to read the story. "Two third graders disproved rumors that the local library is haunted. Abby Spencer and Dakota Marshall uncovered evidence of a flying squirrel."

"It was living in the cellar," Abby said. "It was stealing nuts and cookies!"

Gram nodded. "It says that in the story. I guess it chewed the wiring, too."

"Everyone thought the library was haunted," Abby explained. "But it was only a little squirrel."

"We'll have to cut that story out and frame it," Abby's mom said. "I'm very proud of you!"

Abby blushed. "The best part is that now we can still have the sleepover!" she said.

"Well, we have a few things to do before the sleepover," her mom said. "Tomorrow is Christmas!"

Abby spun around in the middle of the kitchen. "I know! I know!" she cried. "I can hardly wait!" She ran to look out the window.

"Honey, it's not supposed to snow," her mom said.

"Maybe it will," Abby said. "Sometimes the weatherman is wrong."

Her mother laughed. "Yes, sometimes he is. But I think it will be too warm for snow."

Abby shrugged. "It's okay," she said with a grin. "I'm just happy it's almost Christmas!"

Abby spent the day helping her mom. They wrapped presents. They took cookies to the neighbors. Abby put Lucy's special Christmas collar on her. Finally, everything was ready.

Abby's dad came home early from work. They had a special dinner for Christmas Eve. Then they went to church. Abby loved to sing the carols. This year she was allowed to hold her own candle.

They walked out to the parking lot after church. It was dark and cold. Abby looked up at the starry sky.

Her dad gave her a hug. "Still looking for snow?" he asked.

She shook her head. "No," she said. "I'm looking for flying squirrels. I hope the library's squirrel has a warm place to spend Christmas Eve!"

Her dad laughed. "I'm sure he does. He's probably snacking on sunflower seeds from our bird feeder!"

"Time to go home!" said Abby's mom. "Let's have cookies and cocoa before you hang your stocking!"

The Sleepover

The sleepover was four days after Christmas. Abby and Sydney put their sleeping bags into the car. They piled their pillows in the back. They each had a tote with pajamas, slippers, and a toothbrush. They whispered and giggled all the way to the library.

"Do you need help carrying anything in?" Abby's mom asked.

"No, thanks," Abby said.

"Give me a hug," her mom said. "Will you be done at ten tomorrow morning?"

Abby hugged her tight. "Maybe you shouldn't come until ten thirty," she said. "We want to help Mrs. Mackenzie clean up."

"Okay," her mom said. "Have fun!"

Abby and Sydney laughed. "Don't worry, we will!" Abby said.

They picked up their stuff and headed for the library doors. The air felt frosty cold. They could see their breath.

The library was warm and cozy. Abby and Sydney put their things by the window seat in the Children's Area. That was their favorite spot for the sleepover. Every year they curled up there together. They would talk and talk before they fell asleep.

Dakota and Zachary arrived a few minutes later. Abby and Sydney helped put out the snacks and drinks. The boys set up chairs in the program room.

Mrs. Mackenzie had activities planned all evening. First, a magician put on a show. He did a lot of card tricks. Then he showed them an empty box. He tapped it three times and said a magic word.

Three real doves flew out of the box! They circled the room. Their wings flapped in the air. Zachary tried to catch a dove, but it pooped on his head! Everybody laughed!

White stuff dripped off Zachary's hair. "It's not funny!" he protested.

Dakota handed Zachary a napkin. "Just be glad it landed on your head and not the food," he giggled. "Come on. I'll help you wash it off."

The magician tipped his top hat. "I'm so sorry," he told Zachary.

"It's okay," Zachary grumbled. He and Dakota went to the restroom to wash his hair.

The magician caught his doves. He packed up his tricks and went home. Everyone played games after he left.

Then they had a paper hat contest. Everyone made funny hats. Zachary glued gumdrops and candy canes on his. He used it to cover his messy hair. Mrs. Mackenzie gave him a prize for being a good sport.

At ten o'clock, Mrs. Mackenzie served pizza. Then she made popcorn. All the kids went to the program room for a movie.

The evening whizzed by. Everyone had so much fun! Abby ate too much pizza. She was too full to eat any popcorn.

Abby and Sydney put on their pajamas. They lay on the floor to watch the movie. It was so warm and dark. Abby could feel her eyes closing.

She rolled over and looked at Sydney. "Let's go to bed," Abby said. "I'm so sleepy."

"Me too," said Sydney.

They sneaked off to their sleeping bags. Only the light at the circulation desk was still on. The Christmas tree glowed in the center of the room. Its lights twinkled in the dark.

Abby slid into her sleeping bag. "I think that tree is so pretty," she said.

"I love to watch the tree lights when the room is dark," said Sydney.

Abby giggled. "And we don't have to worry about ghosts," she said.

Sydney nodded. "That's a good thing!"

"I wonder where the squirrel is," Abby said.

Sydney glanced out the window. "Abby, look!" she said, pointing.

Great big snowflakes drifted down under the streetlights! The streets and the sidewalks were covered in white. The town of Evergreen looked just like a Christmas card!

Abby jumped up. Suddenly she wasn't sleepy anymore. This was what she had been waiting for all winter! "Snow!" she yelled.

Sydney grinned. "Snow!" she said.

They raced into the program room, jumping over sleepy kids. Abby stood right in front of the movie screen.

"Hey!" Dakota yelled. "I can't see!"

"It's snowing!" Abby yelled. "It's really snowing! There is tons of snow everywhere! Come and see!"

Everyone ran out of the program room. They took turns looking out the windows.

Dakota jumped up and down. "I can use my skis tomorrow!" he said.

Sydney grinned at Abby. "And we can go sledding!"

"And build a snowman!" Abby said.

The snowflakes fell harder and harder. The Christmas lights looked so pretty along the street. The trees and bushes sparkled.

Finally, some kids went back to watch the movie. But Abby and Sydney snuggled into their sleeping bags. They could still see the snow falling even when they were lying down. They could see the library Christmas tree, too.

"This is the best spot!" said Sydney.

Abby smiled. "It is," she said. "And I'm so glad it snowed. This is our best sleepover ever!"

As the snow fell softly, the flying squirrel of Evergreen Library was munching on some nuts in its new home. The Evergreen Zoo was happy to have such an adventurous new addition!

Flying Squirrels

Abby and her friends know they can get lots of information at the library! Mrs. Mackenzie helped them find out some facts about flying squirrels. Evergreen Library's squirrel was a Northern Flying Squirrel.

- Northern Flying Squirrels have reddish-brown fur. Southern Flying Squirrels are gray. Both types of squirrels have white stomachs. They have large, round eyes. Their tails are flat.

- Flying squirrels have extra skin between their front and back legs. This skin allows them to glide when it is stretched out. It looks as though they are flying.

- Flying squirrels do not hibernate. They stay active all winter. They sometimes get into the attics of people's homes.

- Flying squirrels eat acorns, nuts, berries, mushrooms, and seeds.

- Flying squirrels are nocturnal. They only come out at night.